P9-CCQ-917

For baby Eddy

BEACH LANE BOOKS • An imprint of Simon & Schuster Children's Publishing Division • 1230 Avenue of the Americas, New York, New York 10020

• For information about special discounts for bulk purchases, please contact Simon & Schuster Special Sales at 1-866-506-1949 or business@simonandschuster.com. • The Simon & Schuster Speakers Bureau can bring authors to your live event. For more information or to book an event, contact the Simon & Schuster Speakers Bureau at 1-866-248-3049 or visit our website at www.simonspeakers.com. • Book design by Lauren Rille • The text for this book is set in Plumbsky. • Manufactured in China • 0415 SCP • 10 9 8 7 6 5 4 3 2 1 • Library of Congress Cataloging-in-Publication Data • Lester, Alison, author, illustrator. • Noni the pony goes to the beach / Alison Lester. – First edition. • pages cm • Summary: In rhyming text, Noni the pony and her friends, Dave Dog and Coco the cat, spend the day at the beach. • ISBN 978-1-4814-4625-9 (hardcover) – ISBN 978-1-4814-4626-6 (e-book) 1. Ponies–Juvenile fiction. 2. Beaches–Juvenile fiction. 3. Friendship–Juvenile fiction. 4. Stories in rhyme. [1. Stories in rhyme. 2. Ponies–Fiction. 3. Animals–Fiction. 4. Beaches–Fiction. 5. Friendship–Fiction.] I. Title. • PZ8.3.L54935Nr 2015 • [E]–dc23 • 2014043640

Alison Lester

noni the pony goes to the beach

BEACH LANE BOOKS • New York London Toronto Sydney New Delhi

Noni the Pony is friendly and funny
and loves going down to the beach when it's sunny.

With Coco and Dave and the ladies next door,
she slides down the sand dunes and onto the shore.

They frolic and splash as the waves tumble by,
scattering seagulls into the sky.

Dave dives like an arrow into the sea,
as dolphins go dancing by—one, two, and three.

Coco the cat doesn't like getting wet,
so she has a snooze in an old fishing net.

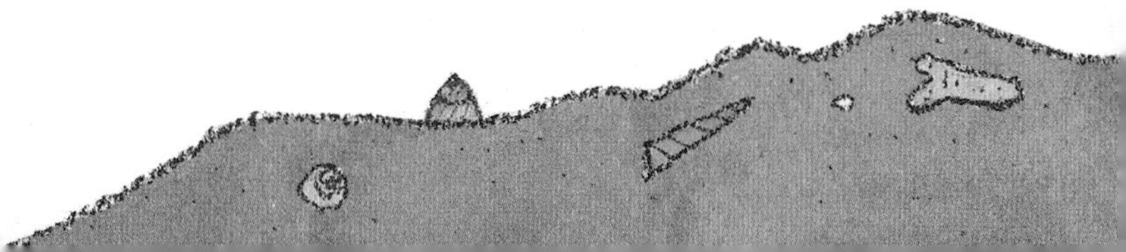

The ladies next door go in up to their knees,
then run to drip-dry in the soft summer breeze.

Instead of a castle, the friends build a boat,
and Dave sets to work on a circular moat.

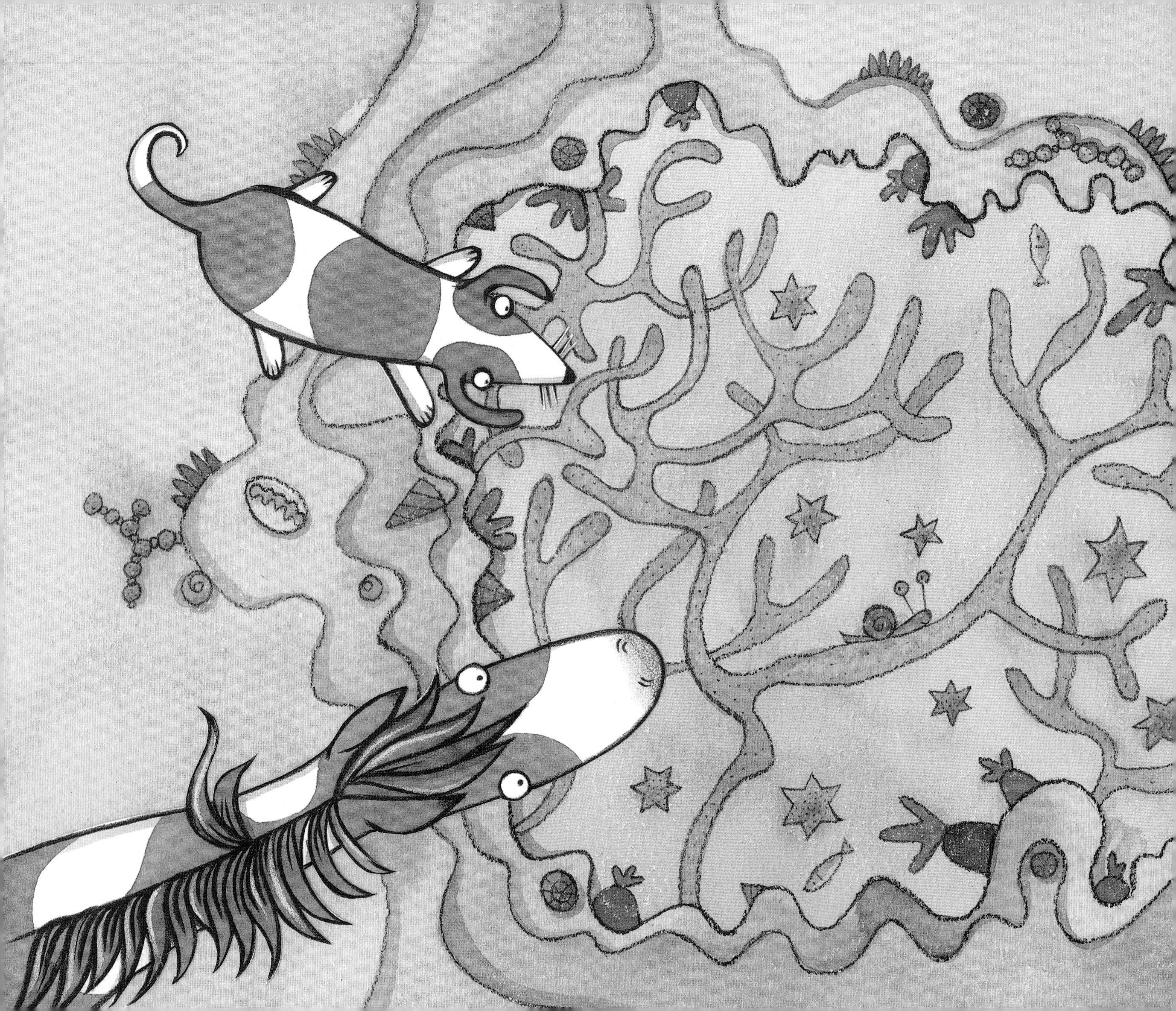

When they peer into a tide pool at one lonely snail,
Coco almost gets nipped on her tail.

Far out to sea, a whale blows her spout.
Dave goes to look, but he swims too far out!

So Noni the Pony, faithful and brave,
wades through the swells and rescues poor Dave.

Then the friends head for home,
up the road from the bay . . .

happy and tired from their wonderful day.